THE COCK IS THE CULPRIT

DESIGN NOTE

The front cover of the novel and the inside illustrations have been designed by Riyas Komu. He is a critically acclaimed multi-media artist, invested in reviving art education and developing art infrastructure in India. Exhibited extensively across India and abroad, his key works focus on archiving the political and cultural history of our time. He conceptualized the Kochi-Muziris Biennale and co-founded the Kochi Biennale Foundation.

UNNI R.

Translated from the Malayalam by J. Devika

VINTAGE
An imprint of Penguin Random House

VINTAGE

USA | Canada | UK | Ireland | Australia
New Zealand | India | South Africa | China | Singapore

Vintage is part of the Penguin Random House group of companies
whose addresses can be found at global.penguinrandomhouse.com

Published by Penguin Random House India Pvt. Ltd
4th Floor, Capital Tower 1, MG Road,
Gurugram 122 002, Haryana, India

Penguin
Random House
India

First published in Malayalam as *Prathi Poovan Kozhi* in 2019
First published in English as *The Cock Is the Culprit* in 2020 by Eka,
an imprint of Westland Publications Private Limited
Published in Vintage by Penguin Random House India 2022

Copyright © Unni R. 2019
Translation copyright © J. Devika 2020
Illustrations: Riyas Komu

ISBN 9780670097470

Typeset by Jojy Philip, New Delhi 110015
Printed at Replika Press Pvt. Ltd, India

www.penguin.co.in

MIX
Paper from
responsible sources
FSC® C016779

This is a legitimate digitally printed version of the book and therefore might not
have certain extra finishing on the cover.

Contents

ONE

Misgivings

*K*ochukuttan had this thing about early mornings— he would lie quietly in bed, half asleep, half awake. That's the hour in which the past arrived unsieved by age, the times, day or night. Weddings, childbirths, deaths, men-women, the goat and the buffalo—all of these would fill his eyes. He'd lie there, gazing at them with eyes from which sleep would be slipping away. He would then get up and walk with them to the shade of the coconut tree. But for some time now, the future had elbowed aside the past in his reveries. And in that future lay the arrival of the passport and the visa, the getting into an aeroplane, and working in Saudi Arabia. In exactly that order. Today, too, he was waiting to get into the aeroplane of the future, when he heard Amma call out: 'Kochuve, eda, I am leaving.'

Kochukuttan got up and walked towards the coconut tree with the aeroplane inside his head. They had a toilet, but he was insistent that the first offering of the day must be made to the coconut tree. As he stepped into the flight cabin, he thought—what will I do every morning in Saudi? They don't have coconut trees, only palm trees ... He'd have to give up his relationship with the coconut tree for a while. Could it be left behind so blithely? It wasn't clear from where the question came, but it came swiftly, as though it had slithered down the tree-trunk. The pee just stopped. This was no ordinary coconut tree. The sapling planted on Amma's father Appuppan's grave had grown into a full-bodied and tall fellow, shaking its leaves about like a hippie's locks. Now fully emptied of sleep, Kochukuttan's eyes climbed up the tree without a *talappu*-belt. Halfway up, the bunches and bunches of coconuts that lay ripening on their stalks told him in Appuppan's voice: I'm stuck here between heaven and earth in so many bunches only so that you can all enjoy your lives! He wasn't sure if he'd actually heard it, or if it was his imagination, but it struck him that he'd been pissing every morning on the old man who'd stayed single-trunked all these years for the sake of his daughter and her son. The thought left him in some discomfort.

Appuppan surfaced again at breakfast. The thoughts about right and wrong too. It was a habit that he had indulged in for years, with no trace of guilt whatsoever—why did it rankle now? Amma used to say often that unthinkable things happen all the time in life. Did unthinkable things also occur in thought? He could not finish the dosa.

When he stepped out of the house for a stroll, he thought—this has probably happened to many people in different times to different degrees. Maybe some of them have built whole philosophical systems out of these thoughts! Anyway, in this case, a sufficient number of theories were already available, and one didn't need to forge yet another. Let Appuppan sitting high above not blight his joyful daily ritual! He was about to decide on placing the request before Appuppan when someone called to him loudly: 'Kochuve!'

It was Kuttappaasaar, the washerman.

'Did you hear?'

Kuttappaasaar was, of course, unaware that Kochukuttan's mind was hung so heavy with thoughts that no other news could possibly enter it. No, he shook his head.

'There's a police jeep at the junction, and they're asking for Naniyamma's house!'

Police, in Naaniyamma's house? That didn't sound real. Kuttapaasaar had walked off by then, so he couldn't ask him anything more.

Naaniyamma lived by herself. She must be nearing ninety now. She cooked just one meal a day. Had a big yard around the house and lots of mango and jackfruit trees—anyone could get some fruits any time. Sometimes relatives came visiting, but such occasions were rare. He had helped her during the thulam showers last year. The roof was leaking, so he had replaced two of the tiles. Maybe something had happened to her … He turned into the lane leading to her house, walking briskly.

There were people who would murder a ninety-year-old woman or despoil her body without a tinge of guilt. Maybe something of that sort … The obscenity of such thoughts struck him as they kept revolving inside his head. Why such ugly thoughts now? He was sure they wouldn't have occurred to him some time back. As he gained pace, nursing the general thought that his thinking was rather disordered these days, a stone struck his backside. He turned to look. It was Ambika chechi, of the Tekkethil house.

'I've been calling out to you for so long! Where are you running off to?'

'No place in particular,' Kochukuttan lied.

'But where are you off to?'

'Naaniyamma's. The police is there.'

'Ayyo!' she exclaimed, stupefied. Kochukuttan didn't stop. Stopping meant chatting with her. And that meant letting her persuade him to repair her tap, which would then extend to washing down the tiles of her roof. So he ran. When he slowed down, he realised that his thoughts had not been running with him. Or were they testing him, to see how far he'd run? Suppressing such intellectual dilemmas for the moment, he turned to face the immediate empirical reality. The police jeep was parked at the gate of the house. The sub-inspector stood leaning against it. Two policemen stood further away. Another policeman was walking around the house, shouting, 'Anyone home?'

'Saar, it seems there's no one in there,' he shouted.

'Look again, carefully,' suggested the SI, walking over towards him.

The boundary between Naaniyamma's house and the road was a row of dilapidated thatches put up a very long time ago. You had to walk through the yard to reach the house. A path shaped out of people's footfalls winded down it, like a moulted snakeskin. On either side of the path grew shameplants, false daisies, heart-leaf sida plants, and many others.

Kochukuttan tried smiling at the policeman who was standing there, but the policeman did not smile back.

'There's someone in the toilet outside the house, it looks like,' said the policeman.

'Will they be out anytime soon?'

'Will take time if they are constipated.'

The SI hmm-ed. Tapioca lay drying on a mat outside. He picked up a few pieces and began to munch.

'What's the matter, saar?' asked Kochukuttan of the unsmiling policeman.

'You'll fix it, huh, if you knew?' he snapped back.

Kochukuttan said nothing and stepped back. He could hear the anxious heartbeats of the people who had gathered there. He alone couldn't hold his anxiety back; it tipped over. That was why he had to take the policeman's bark.

Naaniyamma never went anywhere. She must be inside. Her hearing was poor. You just have to go right in. The suggestions were pushing and shoving each other on the tip of Kochukuttan's tongue when they heard the sound of something shuffling in the sand at the back of the house. After some time, Naaniyamma came out. The sound stopped.

She paid no attention to the people standing in her yard. She dropped the coconut frond she was dragging and sat down beside it.

'Hey,' the policeman tried to call.

She did not look at him. The policeman squatted next to her and said, 'We have to ask you something.'

Naaniyamma began to weave the fronds.

'Saar, she can't hear,' someone in the crowd said. The driver of the police jeep turned to look. All the faces he saw bore the same mien.

'Saare, she is a *potti*! Stone-deaf!' the driver called out.

Kochukuttan did not like the expression *potti*, but he kept quiet.

As he walked back with the policeman, the SI asked the crowd, 'Which one is P.K. Chandrasenan Nair's house?'

They exchanged puzzled looks. They were hearing the name for the first time.

A policeman tried to share the little bit he knew: 'Both sons are abroad …'

Ah! Now you're making sense—Chaakku, you mean! The crowd of tongues gathered there itched to say that, but instead, all their fingers pointed towards the house beyond the massive wall that bounded Naaniyamma's yard.

That the paunchy and bald Chaakku, who liked to pretend he was taller than that wall, had such a fancy long name was news to them. The chap had married Vadakkel Krishnankutty Nair's older sister, claiming to be an army man. Many were surprised—how did this man who was barely four-and-a-half feet ever get into the army? Because Krishnankutty Nair's family used to be big guns in those parts then, the surprise went in and out of a few ears, and then disappeared. But it was Mathai, the owner of the ration-shop, who dug out a pet-name that one of the groom's less important guests had left behind on the wedding-day: Chaakku. He distributed it liberally to all the folk who came to his shop to get rice and sugar.

Some of those who sought out the origins of the name came to the conclusion that he wasn't in the army but was actually a sack-dealer in Kunnamkulam—that he sold *chaakku*, gunny-bags, for a living! Others disputed this information. Be that as it may, when he returned with a pretty pile of cash, the first thing he did was to build that huge wall. To those who were astonished by its height, Chaakku's brother-in-law Krishnankutty Nair clarified that it was meant for protection from enemies. Enemies? People continue to be astonished even now.

The SI went into the house alone.

Chaakku's wife opened the door. After a while, Chaakku arrived.

The SI asked him, 'She's a *potti*, right?'

'Oh, that's her stunt!'

'How do we question the hag at her age? Do something, saar,' suggested the SI.

'What?' Chaakku's face looked pinched.

'Just put her down,' suggested the SI.

'Kill her?' Chaakku felt a tiny nip of fear.

'My dear saar, that's the easiest …!'

'But … then, this …'

'I'll take care of the rest.'

Chaakku looked straight at the SI's face. Catching the promise of the promise he'd just made, he nodded.

When the jeep disappeared beyond the turn of the road past Chaakku's house and could no longer be heard, the people hanging around the place came together. It was evident from their faces that they were all equally worried at not being in the know of things.

'Kochuve, why don't you go ask him what the matter is?' someone said.

Before he could ask why someone else couldn't volunteer, another person added, 'If any of us ask, he'll just beat around the bush. But he'll tell *you*.'

Why should that be? Kochukuttan had no clue. But in that moment, he misconstrued the situation, thinking that he was the sole hope of all those who were gathered there. Based on that understanding, he reached Chaakku's doorstep.

He knock-knocked on the door a couple of times. When he raised his hand for the third time, the door swung open abruptly. No word came out of Chaakku's mouth; the question was evident in his face.

Kochukuttan folded his hands respectfully. Chaakku did not return the gesture. Kochukuttan smiled. Chaakku did not.

'Just came over to ask why the police were here,' Kochukuttan said courteously.

'The police know why they were here—won't that do?'

'No, not that. Just about Naaniyamma. They said they wanted to ask her something.'

'I am being civil, telling you this much,' said Chaakku, half closing the door. 'So, be on your way!'

'Naaniyamma is a harmless woman. If you try anything with her, you'll learn a lesson for sure.'

Chaakku hadn't expected that retort. Kochukuttan hadn't planned it either. The two surprises held them both still for a few moments.

When he came out, those who were waiting outside, near the wall, came together again.

'What's up?' the crowd asked. The question seemed to rise from one throat.

Kochukuttan looked at them but did not utter a word. He turned away and began to walk off. How did I find the balls to hit back like that? He thought hard, but the answer eluded him.

TWO

Old Chalk-dust

*W*hy did Chaakku call the police? Naaniyamma had no relatives; she was as alone as a single-trunk coconut tree. She'd done neither good nor evil to the local folk. What complaint, then, could Chaakku have against her? And even if he did have something, was calling the police the way to resolve it? What was this big, unresolvable problem anyway? Chaakku's brother-in-law, Krishnankutty Nair, overheard many such questions as he sat in the little shed just behind the ration-shop.

Chaakku was Krishnankutty's brother-in-law, but he still thought that Chaakku was a jerk. Because he could guess how the person who had tried to ask Chaakku about the matter would have been treated, he was at a loss.

'Did you know? He grabbed Kochu by the throat and pushed him!' That was the ration-shop-keeper, Mathai.

'Really?' asked Krishnankutty.

'But of course!'

As he tripped on many contradictory thoughts like concern for his sister's future, the smugness of the know-it-all in him, Chaakku's long-standing contempt for his lowly school-master-status ... someone said from outside the shed: 'Tell your brother-in-law not to twist and tangle needlessly.'

Krishnankutty knew what lay behind that mild threat. So, without wasting any more words, he replied, 'Yes, I will talk to him.'

Anticipating the danger involved in meeting his brother-in-law alone, he got Kurup saar to go with him. Kurup saar was very popular. He was a revolutionary who had eventually converted to piety and bhakti. A person who believed that he would have to worship in every puja, from nirmaalyam at early dawn to athaazapuja at night in order to exorcise the memories of his past. Mathai tagged along without asking either of them.

Oblivious of the fact that things were beginning to roll and gather like storm-clouds, Kochukuttan had shut himself inside his room and was engaged in a close analysis of all the happenings since that morning. On one side, his personal dilemmas. On the other side, the police, and that rich man Chaakku, who held everything and everyone from refugees to animals and birds in deep contempt, and his hubris-filled words that tried to decimate a question that had sprouted from human concern. Two mutually-opposed questions were lined up before Kochukuttan, one facing the other. He tried to figure out which one to address first. After calm contemplation, he felt that he had to stand with justice.

Noting the displeasure on Chaakku's face when he saw Mathai with them, Krishnankutty was convinced that this would not be easy. He therefore opened the conversation saying that Kurup saar had something to discuss. Well, in that case, he could do the talking himself, said Chaakku, holding up a warning sign right at the start and asking them, quite formally, to be seated.

Kurup saar counted to two after they sat down and asked directly, 'What really happened?'

Knowing well that the story about Naaniyamma must have been served at different scales and in different measures, and according to diverse tastes, in a variety of places ranging from the *kavala*—the junction where the roads crossed—to toddy-shops and homes, from this morning until now, Chaakku launched a counter-question: 'Tell me what you have heard …?'

'That the police came to nab Naaniyamma,' Krishnan-kutty said.

'And?'

'Kochu was grabbed by his throat and pushed.'

'Who said that?'

Kurup saar's eyes turned towards Mathai.

'I overheard it in the *kavala*,' said Mathai, having instantly become a warrior of justice.

Chaakku fell silent for a few moments.

'It's true.' His booming voice shook the room briefly.

Then he fell silent again. As the silence grew longer, Kurup saar drew upon his venerable age and the special rights he enjoyed as a revered personage in the locality to whisper a few words: 'We haven't been told what it is.'

Spying a whole crowd of people behind these three and their evenly-creased foreheads, all bearing the same question, Chaakku said, 'It isn't something that can be discussed in public.'

Mathai alone didn't grasp the hint that Chaakku was interested only in a conversation in which Mathai wouldn't be included.

Krishnankutty and Kurup saar looked at each other. It was all right to exclude a third person when a secret was waiting, ready to expose itself to them. They communicated this to each other via that look.

Chaakku sensed this and got up from his chair. When Krishnankutty and Kurup saar stood up, Mathai got up too, but Chaakku gestured to him to sit down.

The two men followed Chaakku into another room, and the door was shut behind them. Mathai was left alone on the verandah. That he was left out of the secret made him feel breathless; he struggled to cope with the feeling. But he managed to catch a few words and some mysterious sounds that crept out through the keyhole of the closed door. None of them came out as a proper sentence. And the ones that squeezed themselves out did not form themselves into meaning; they lay separate and distinct, forming masses of tiny islets of words. In the end, a question came out of the room along with Chaakku's rumbling voice and forceful tone: 'Now you tell me, was I wrong in doing it?'

Mathai couldn't catch Krishnankutty's or Kurup saar's responses. After some time, the door opened and the three of them came out. Mathai thought the faces of the two other than Chaakku looked swollen from the secret. Kurup saar went off without even bidding goodbye. Krishnankutty left without even bothering to ask after his sister. And after them, Mathai too went away, his heart heavy.

On the way back, he did begin to ask a couple of times about what had transpired in there, but desisted, fearing that he might be unable to bear the weight of the secret that Krishnankutty and Kurup saar were carrying.

When the dusk grew into night, they reached the turning towards their respective homes.

'What to say if anyone asks?' Mathai asked, as helpless as someone holding an empty bowl. To this, Kurup saar replied, 'Just maintain a grave silence.'

Krishnankutty and Mathai went to their respective homes. Kurup saar alone headed for Kochukuttan's house.

'Where are you going after such an early dinner?' Kochukuttan's mother Sumathi asked as she served him pieces of roasted dried fish.

'Just for a walk,' he said. Sumathi sensed that his mind was elsewhere.

She said, 'Either eat or think what you are thinking. If you do both together, you won't taste the food, and the thinking won't be good either.'

It was Amma's occasional lessons in philosophy that kept Kochukuttan's back straight. He sometimes wondered whether his feelings, doubts and other such things did not sprout from these tiny bits of wisdom. He liked what she said, and was getting ready to set his thoughts aside and enjoy the roasted fish, when he heard someone calling him: 'Kochuve!'

'You sit there,' said Amma. 'I'll see who's at the door.'

Finding Kurup saar at the door, she asked, 'Why, saar! This is unusual ...'

'Is Kochu home?'

'He's having dinner. Please be seated, saar.'

Saar sat on the parapet in the verandah.

'Shall I make some black tea?'

No, he gestured, and asked, 'Has his visa arrived?'

'No. The money's ready. Have to pay this week.'

'Saudi, right?'

Sumathi nodded.

'Better to pay after the passport comes?'

'Oh, it should be coming anytime now. But they want the money sooner.'

'Let him escape and make a life instead of loitering around here.'

Sumathi nodded again.

Kochukuttan burped as he entered the verandah. Seeing Kurup saar, he guessed the reason for this unexpected visit. Kurup saar also guessed that Kochukuttan had guessed it. He got up.

'We are going down to the steps at the gate,' Kurup saar said, walking out, towards the darkness. Kochukuttan followed him. Sumathi went back inside.

'Ahem,' said Kurup saar, trying to start formally. 'See, we should not talk without knowing the truth—so it's important to separate the right from the wrong.'

Kochukuttan didn't have the patience to listen to Kurup saar's homilies, and so he picked up a sentence that was written a very long while ago in chalk on the ceiling of the library and put it before him. It was a line from *The Good Person of Szechwan*:

What sort of city is this?

What sort of people are you?

When injustice is done there should be revolt in the city.

If there's no revolt,

It were better that the city should perish before the night falls...

'If there is injustice in a city, there should be revolts there. If not, it is better for it to be burned to the ground.'

Kurup saar was dumbstruck by that response. Then, recovering, he asked innocently, 'But Kochu, we live in a village, don't we? This isn't a town!'

Kochukuttan wasn't around to hear him.

Kurup saar tried hard to rub off the whitish old chalk-powder from his hands.

THREE

Sarcasm

When Sumathi stepped out to sweep the yard, Ponnamma from next door was pacing up and down uneasily, not sure whether to ask or not to ask. Her husband Narayanan was nudging her to ask. Will Sumathi erupt if I ask; Ponnamma's anxiety was about *that*. And it made her pace up and down and back again. When she noticed that Sumathi was done sweeping, Ponnamma's curiosity exploded and she leapt towards the fence in the backyard.

'Sumathiii…' she called.

Sumathi had heaped up the dry leaves in a corner and was preparing to burn them. She turned around.

'Is it true, what we heard?'

'What did you hear?'

'That the police hauled off our Kochu at midnight?'

Sumathi nodded as she continued her task. Ponnamma stood there for a bit and then, squeezing herself through the fence, went up to Sumathi.

'Why did they take him?'

'Nothing about a girl. He stuck some stuff on that Chaakku's wall, that's what …'

'Did they beat him up or what?'

'If they beat him, I'll get him massaged and treated. Or feed him half-boiled eggs. What else?'

When the stink of burning plastic began to spread, Sumathi started walking away from it towards the kitchen. Ponnamma followed.

'Has someone gone to bail him out?'

'Jaleel, his father, and some others have gone.'

Sumathi stepped into the kitchen. A lid that rested on top of the rice-pot was rising and falling, as if gasping for breath.

'It's been an hour since I put it on, and it's still not cooked! Tough grains!'

Ponnamma didn't respond to that observation.

'Why does he get caught up in such unnecessary things—what a pity!' Ponnamma said, expressing her sorrow. She closed the kitchen-door lightly.

As though she had been waiting for the regret to bubble up, Sumathi turned sharply and strode up to Ponnamma.

'All right, so what else should he have done?'

'No, no,' said Ponnamma, frightened, moving back a step.

'All of you creep into Naaniyamma's yard to get kokum, drumsticks and what not. How much money did you all filch off her when her head was clearer? And when the police went there, you knew, but did any of you—you, your man, or—yes, haven't you got four-five strapping fellows, growing taller and taller like barren and useless coconut trees—did any of you bother to go there and find out? And now you're blaming my boy!'

'My dear Sumathi, that isn't what I said,' Ponnamma said, trying to lower her voice.

'Not like your oldest fellow, crawling all over the temple grounds at festivals, grabbing women's asses,' finished Sumathi, before she went into another room and fetched a poster to show Ponnamma. She flung it at her. Ponnamma could read the red letters on the blue paper only hazily.

Sumathi read aloud the slogan: Protest against the conspiracy to foist a false case on Naaniyamma! He had left this copy behind because of a spelling mistake. When she found out that the police had nabbed her son on account of this piece of evidence, Sumathi could well see why he was dragged off.

Ponnamma nodded and was about to sneak off without even a goodbye when an autorickshaw arrived at the gate. It was Kochukuttan. Jaleel and his father were with him. Ponnamma would have loved to stay and enquire about the arrest, but the atmosphere didn't seem too congenial. And so she retreated into her own country through the gap in the fence.

'You can go now,' said Kochukuttan.

'No, only after some tea,' Sumathi called out to them.

'We'll go after you have a bath,' Jaleel's father suggested.

Kochukuttan lost his balance a bit as he was climbing the rough-cut steps of the house. Sumathi ran up to him.

'Were you standing the whole night … You need some sleep.'

Kochukuttan went to his room. Sumathi decided to skip work that day.

The right to protest is a fundamental right of all citizens, male or female. Kochukuttan's only fault was that he exercised it. If someone protests when the police suddenly close in on an old lady who lives all alone, and the complainant refuses to reveal the reason for complaining, that is a positive indicator of the freedom that citizens enjoy in a democracy. If the person who protested is pointed out to the police and they arrest him in violation of his rights, that can only be evidence of a dictatorial tendency. It is particularly condemnable when such an act is perpetrated by someone so venerable in age and knowledge. To trap a young man getting ready to work abroad in such a case is nothing less than destroying his dreams. Therefore we demand that the reasons for the personal enmity shown towards Naaniyamma be revealed post-haste. Also, the case filed against Kochukuttan must be withdrawn immediately.

When Chaakku crumpled and flung away this statement that the Citizens' Forum had prepared, Krishnankutty, taking note of the pitiful state of the piece of paper and also the murderous rage on his brother-in-law's face, told him: 'Aliya, this is going to go far. It won't end where we want it to end.'

Chaakku didn't get what he was hinting at.

'You've been illegally filling up ten whole paras of paddy fields. On top of that, you've encroached on the panchayat road while building this house … people know of it. If anyone digs it up, there will be a resurvey. The work on the paddy land will be stayed. So, really, do you want a run-in with the locals?'

Chaakku was silent for some time.

Then he asked, 'So what are you leading up to, Krishnankutty?'

'Withdraw the complaint against the boy. And tell people what's going on with Naaniyamma.'

'I can withdraw the complaint. But what about the other thing? That's going to affect national security!'

A female voice from inside the house reminded him that he should first take care of his own security before worrying about national security. Chechi opens her mouth rarely, thought Krishnankutty, but when she does, she thulps you.

The refusal to give in, on one side; so much illegal stuff, on the other. When it struck him that small defeats can lead to large victories, Chaakku realised that one must view these not as surrender but as appropriate tactics. He nodded in such a way that Krishnankutty could see that it was precisely such a realisation that was swinging left and right inside Chaakku's head.

Krishnankutty informed him of the Citizens' Forum's decision to meet him at the SNDP Yogam hall late that afternoon. Chaakku did not conceal his discomfort at having to forego his siesta. 'What's wrong with meeting now?'

'Kochu is sleeping. He's the defendant, right? Let him wake up and then we will meet—that's what they are saying.'

Chaakku nodded. But before Krishnankutty stepped out, he made another attempt. 'Do we have to meet in *their* hall? Why not meet at the Nair Karayogam?'

'It doesn't have a ceiling fan,' said Krishnankutty.

Chaakku sat before Krishnankutty, Kurup saar, Mathai, members of various political parties who had come together to form the Citizens' Forum, Kochukuttan, and some fifty other people, like a lone warrior facing a whole army. Since no introduction or prayer was called for, Kurup saar ended the confusion about how to start by announcing 'Let us begin' with a shake of his head. Chaakku made the first offering: 'I am withdrawing the complaint against Sri Kochukuttan.'

The room rang with the applause of everyone except Kochukuttan. When it stopped, he spoke up: 'Before that, the complaint against Naaniyamma must be dropped.'

Chaakku looked at Krishnankutty and Kurup saar. Kurup saar got up and said in his naturally mild voice, 'Naaniyamma is a good woman. No one has any doubt about that. But one is not sure if the rooster in her house has the same goodness of character.'

There was a general sense of puzzlement all around.

'It's only natural that when one files a complaint against a rooster, it becomes a complaint against its owner.'

The audience continued to gawp.

'Mr Chandrasenan Nair has had an experience with Naaniyamma's rooster that may strike you as really odd, but it is one that poses a serious threat to our national security and is indeed a blot on our national pride. That is why he had to file such a case.'

Now the audience seemed to be not only taken aback, but also genuinely worried. Kurup saar sat down. Chaakku got up to speak:

'Two days back, some ten or fifteen of us had gathered in the frontyard of my house to honour the sacred memory of our martyrs and discuss the threats raised by terrorism. We had decided to begin with a silent prayer. All of us stood up and closed our eyes to pray. Suddenly, there was a sharp crowing. Surprised by such a sharp sound, our eyes opened involuntarily! We then saw a rooster on the boundary wall. I have seen it before many times. It had never encroached into our premises. I had never ever heard it crow, either. And yes, this same rooster was behaving thus, in such an unprecedented way! Go away, you fowl—we first yelled at it politely. But no. Not only did it refuse to leave, it kept crowing louder and louder. In short, a day set apart for sacred memories and thoughts was lost to crowing and screeching. My complaint was against this utterly unusual crowing. I thought it was necessary to have it investigated. The truth is this. And other than this, I haven't complained against the old lady, nor do I want to trouble her in her ripe old age.'

When Chaakku ended his speech, some people were torn between many things: What to say now? What is the truth? And where is the lie in this? Where are we right now? Others were sceptical—what conspiracy could possibly lurk behind a cock's crowing?

While they were taking their time to emerge from the complexity of the situation, Kurup saar asked, 'Now tell us, should Chaakku withdraw the complaint or not?'

When that plunged most of the audience into yet another dilemma, Kochukuttan alone raised his nose and mouth towards reason and logic, trying to breathe.

All the others agreed that it was only fair to lodge a complaint against a creature that let out an ugly sound when the sacred memory of the brave martyrs of the nation was being evoked. Naaniyamma became irrelevant before the glory of the nation.

As they were about to leave, Chaakku revealed yet another detail: 'That rooster is still crowing. Full of sarcasm. If you strain your ears, you can hear it.'

No one had anticipated such a revelation.

FOUR

Experience

Chaakku was one of those who had celebrated Saddam Hussein's execution by cooking a nice, sweet payasam at home. He had burst crackers when the US invaded Afghanistan. Kochukuttan had heard from some of Chaakku's hangers-on that he believed that the road to peace lay through war. In that case, there lived inside him a fan of the US of A. If he did indeed conduct a silent prayer for fallen soldiers, it could well have been in the memory of American soldiers. Nobody had asked him: which army, which jawans? He had also hidden it cunningly. Kochukuttan felt that this was his way of getting over the disappointment of building a wall so high for fear of enemies and then not finding even a tiny foe anywhere nearby.

Anyone with some common sense should have been able to see that there is no fixed time for cocks to crow.

There's never been a dawn that did not brighten because the cock failed to crow. Neither the mornings nor the sun have suffered any loss because of omissions on the part of cockerels. One or two backyards, the branches of a few trees, a life constantly insecure, even if saved from Sundays and guests for lunch, perpetually in threat from a hand lunging at it from behind—that's probably all that would go into a rooster's biography. How foolish was it, seeing a conspiracy in this? Why, then, was he not able to oppose it at the meeting? Because of cowardice, or the fear of opposing a majority view? Or the feeling that it would be impossible to convince the crowd with reason and logic? The complaint against Naaniyamma still stood because he had been silent. His silence also ensured that the complaint against him would be withdrawn. He could not help thinking that this was an unjust decision; it kept replaying inside his head, finding a place in the list of guilt-ridden feelings there. He resolved to put it before Kurup saar first and then to the Citizens' Forum, which had sprouted up the very next day. But even then, he could not sleep. He stood by the window, staring into the darkness outside till sleep arrived and took him along.

Nobody could believe it at first. It was none other than Kurup saar who said it. He was stingy with words usually; never said anything he couldn't vouch for. A sense of disbelief first put up some resistance, but Kochukuttan's trust in Kurup saar pulled it out by its roots. Those who heard it from him spread it in homes, in the *kavala*s by the roads, in school, in the bathing-ghat by the river. The story was carried to many other places from there. One of these tales made its way to Kochukuttan's house through Mariyamma, who came to deliver milk. Mariyamma, who sounded like a man, called, 'Ente Sumathiye!', and that woke Kochukuttan up. Though separated by a wall, he could make out what she was telling his mother.

'My dear Sumathi, the priest had just started to ring the bell for the morning's nirmaalyapuja—yes, early, before it was light—and there started the crowing! A cock! The poor tirumeni was so scared he started ringing the bell out loud—and it went all kini-kini-kini … Kurup saar looked around—it wasn't yet light, so he couldn't see a thing! What a sound! Like it was screeching right under your ear! The tirumeni put the bell down and somehow uttered the mantras, and was trying to wrap it all up quickly—but what was the use? It was crowing non-stop!'

Sumathi stared at her in complete disbelief.

'*Padchonaane satyam*! I swear on Allah! This morning when I went to Kurup saar's house with the milk, there was quite a crowd there. I heard it there, with—look—these very ears of mine! Saar never says anything false.'

Yes, that's true. Kochukuttan nodded his head, still lying in bed.

He well knew that this crowing in the wee hours of dawn must have, by now, reached countless ears. That made the prospect of a conversation with Kurup saar decidedly dim. Surely, not one cock but many cocks could crow at daybreak? If the cock's hour of crowing coincided with the hour of the nirmaalyapuja, then it was quite possible that this was also the hour of its morning ablutions. Someone as eminent as Kurup saar ought to have thought about this for sure. Did he distribute this unbelievable experience this morning through many tongues without considering this possibility?

He did not feel like getting up. Fatigue, like you might feel when climbing up and down a winding staircase, assailed him. It forced his body to stay prone. At some point in between, he heard his mother call out to him that she was leaving.

Chaakku, who rarely left his home, was seen rather early that day at the roadside *kavala*. People gathered around him from all sides.

'What is to be done?' someone asked.

'Let's wait till evening.'

No one asked why that should be. They were certain that there was some good reason.

'Evening—when would that be?' A doubt stuck its neck out.

'Just before nightfall.'

Noticing the bewilderment on people's faces, Chaakku congratulated himself for his ability to convey an air of mysterious concealment through his words.

When he left, preparations began at the *kavala* for the long and painstaking wait until nightfall. Kochukuttan couldn't muster the courage to tell these anxious minds to pause a moment to think. He went towards Kurup saar's house with questions stifling and choking within him.

The questions, analyses and possibilities that had arisen in the context of the crowing incident—Kochukuttan began to feel lighter when he had set down before Kurup saar the entire burden that he had borne until then. Kurup saar had begun to shake his head when Kochukuttan had started speaking, and continued to do so even after he had finished. Kochukuttan paused, hoping for a more rational response. In the end, in a voice matured with age, Kurup saar replied: 'Your talk is aided by Reason. I am relying on my experience.'

When Kochukuttan walked back home, it was as if his legs had been tied down somewhere. When someone claimed that they had seen God, that was a counter to scientific reason. So what is stronger? Someone's experience? Or rational thought? His legs did not take him home but towards Velachi's toddy-shaap. He entered the place feeling fatigued.

It was already dusk, but no one was to be seen. 'Where's everyone?' he asked.

'They're all at Chaakku's place.'

Kochukuttan gulped down a whole potent bottle and then opened the thatched partition behind the shop to take a look. It was time—dusk was fast fading into night.

He downed three or four more bottles. In the hazy stupor that followed, lying facedown on the desk inside the shaap, he heard snatches of conversation.

'The evening worship was on at the Goddess's sacred grove, our kaavu, and there goes the cock again!'

'Non-stop?'

'Of course, how else? No one knows where it was crowing from. They couldn't see anything in the dark. They could only hear the sound.'

'And?'

'And they managed to somehow wind up the puja!'

'How awful!'

'Yeah, awful, really terrible!'

'Now what are we to do?'

'That's what everyone asked Kurup saar and Chaakku. Chaakku didn't open his mouth. Kurup saar said: *Unmoolanam.* Annihilation.'

'What on earth is that?'

'Something to do with cocks, I suppose.'

FIVE

Darkness

*T*he news spread by older people, that something terrible was about to happen, was quick to infect the children. They began to feel afraid. When was it going to happen? And where? At school? Or while walking back home? No one told them that there was nothing to fear— not the adults at home, not their teachers. Some children came down with fever at the sight of roosters crossing the village paths. Some began to wail and scream. The poor innocent birds were confounded.

In the discussions about the impending catastrophe, Ramachandran, who lived near the pond, hit upon an important question: Yes, danger was on the way, but who was it going to target?

His audience was baffled.

'Just observe: which are the places subjected to the crowing?'

Before he could finish, the rest was fully thought out. The hurry caused a close circle to form. The circle dispersed after taking a decision to warn all the womenfolk at home about the danger.

By then, it was nearly noon.

Ravuther had entered the mosque wondering why Mammath hadn't given the call for prayer. Finding him lying flat on his back staring at the ceiling, he quickly sprinkled water on his face, hoping to rouse him. When Mammath did not revive, Ravuther raised an alarm and people came running. They too tried sprinkling water. Some people lifted him up to take him to hospital. And then he moved his lips: Alhamdulillah!

Those who had hurried back to their homes heard the story on the way: Mammath was getting ready to give the call for prayer. Just when he was starting, he sensed some movement behind him and turned around. And there it was, a rooster flying down towards him! Already shocked into a daze, Mammath saw it alight beside him, spread it wings and raise its head to emit a massive crowing call! The piercing sound was like a blow that knocked Mammath unconscious.

'I won't believe this, Jaleel,' said Kochukuttan.

'Don't, then! My vaappa was standing just outside the mosque. He felt a gust of wind from inside it. So forceful it was, he was pushed to the wall behind him!'

'What wind?'

'The wind from the rooster flying out of the mosque!'

'My dear Jaleel … please, you too? No, don't say this!'

'You think my vaappa's a liar?'

Jaleel's father was a very good man. He was known to have blood pressure issues—when it dropped, or when he had ear problems, he was known to have had minor falls. On those occasions, no one had mentioned a cock or the wind. When Kochukuttan fell silent, Jaleel asked, 'Why aren't you saying anything?'

Nothing. Kochukuttan shook his head.

All human beings have the inborn ability to tell a tale. Some write it down; some just tell it. Those who write the tales are praised as novelists or short-story writers; those who tell them are counted as liars. Because all tales are lies in the final analysis, Kochukuttan felt that this cock and its crowing was a modern folktale. All the local folk were characters in it. More than a tale, it was a large stage on which the characters moved, like a moving-image. Seen that way, this was not a big deal, he thought as he walked alongside Jaleel. And that's when they saw Maryamma chedathy's daughter, Rosamma, and the cooperative society office clerk, Sindhu, running somewhere.

'What's up, Rosammo? *Enna?*' Jaleel called out to her.

'There's big trouble near the school,' Rosamma yelled back, without stopping.

Jaleel ran ahead; Kochukuttan followed him. When they reached the school ground, they found that a large crowd had gathered there. The children had not yet gone home.

'My dear George saar, please tell me, what's the matter?' Sushilan, a panchayat member, was pleading.

'The students were standing on the verandah, as they do every evening, singing the national anthem ...' Before he could finish, the headmaster's throat dried up. Someone ran up with a glass of water. He drank a mouthful and continued: 'They had got past singing *Punjab, Sindh, Gujarat* ... and ... then a piercing hoot ...!'

Jaleel looked at Kochukuttan. Kochukuttan didn't wait to listen to the rest of it; he walked away. After a little while, he heard someone call his name, and turned around.

It was Rosamma. And Sindhu, holding her hand.

'Edo, what's the use of having people like you here?' she asked.

Rosamma's accusation hurt him more than the blows of the police.

'*Enna*, Rosamme, why do you say that?'

'That cock is making everybody's life miserable. Can't you get rid of the whole thing by doing what Kurup saar suggested?'

'Doing what?'

'*Unmoolanam*. Annihilation. Extermination.'

He wanted to say that he did not believe in the theory of extermination, but the words wouldn't emerge from his mouth. Instead, he nodded a yes.

It was decided that they could not let the cock go on like this, and that it should be killed right away. Chaakku gave detailed instructions to each volunteer group about where they should go and where they should search. He especially recommended six-battery torches though they were nearly extinct. They were to set out only after midnight. He drew the finish line too: before the early morning worship, the nirmaalyapuja.

'Aren't you going to catch the roosters?' asked Sumathi.

'I am a bit confused,' replied Kochukuttan.

'Then catch some sleep ...'

Was it right to be sleeping on a night when everybody else was out to catch a common foe? Is this cock and its crowing affecting me in any real sense, he thought. If not, why's that? It's only natural for a patriot, a believer, to feel hurt when their faith is under attack. To crow and hoot instead of engaging in a democratic debate is downright vulgar. That too, by staying hidden away and imitating a cock. This is not a guerrilla tactic. Furthermore, all the blame is piling up on poor Naaniyamma's head. Because she couldn't hear, Naaniyamma was like a planet in another galaxy, revolving around other suns. In such a context, was it not important to devote one's night-time efforts to the task of establishing her innocence?

At midnight, Kochukuttan stepped out all alone. Since the hunt was to begin in Naaniyamma's yard, he made his way there.

He looked inside—the house was defenceless, lacking the protective sheath of light—through an open window on the south-side. There sat Naaniyamma on a cot, dusting old framed photographs.

Kochukuttan called to her: 'Durgadeviye …!' Yes, that was her name—his mother had told him so. Her father had spent some time in north India. All Sumathi knew about it was that it was the name of a woman who had helped a certain young man flee by pretending to be his wife. Actually, it was the name of the revolutionary who had helped Bhagat Singh flee Lahore after assassinating the British police official John Saunders, and had repeatedly given the all-powerful British police the slip. He had lived till the ripe old age of ninety-two. Neither Kochukuttan nor anybody else in that little corner of the world knew anything of it. The local folk knew her only as Naaniyamma, the name her mother called her by, cold and insipid as rice-gruel. And so, the fiery and elusive Durgadevi had to be content with confinement in the ration-card. Earlier, when she could still hear a little, she had given him a betel-stained smile whenever Kochukuttan called her by that name. As her hearing grew weaker and weaker, the smile disappeared.

Though he knew she wouldn't hear it, he called her by that name one more time. Unexpectedly, she turned around.

'It's me, Sumathi's boy.'

No sign of recognition—no word or nod—came from her. But her eyes held his.

'Do you have any idea what's been going on here?'

There was no response.

'Things are in a real twist. And your cock is responsible for all the mess, Naaniyamme!'

Naaniyamma turned her face away and continued to wipe the glass frames. For his own peace of mind, Kochukuttan said, 'It's been affecting the local folk and our village. They've decided to finish it off. Please don't be angry with me.'

As she laid the cleaned photos on the bed, Kochukuttan noticed one, mostly faded, of a moustachioed man. He'd never seen it before. He craned his neck to get a better view. The yellowish light inside the room and the yellowed photo together spirited the image away from sight. But the moustache could be seen clearly. Who was this man? Her father? Or her husband? Or …? Hey, no, no chance at all, he decided—and erased the man who had just climbed in from some history book.

As he was walking away from the house, slower than darkness itself, he sensed something move. The life that had moved was crushed between Kochukuttan's hands in less than a second, before it could let out even a tiny cheep, and then it sank into absolute darkness.

SIX

The Blunder

*I*n the morning, people curious to see the offending cock gathered in front of the panchayat office. When they actually saw the bird, which had grown bigger than an ostrich in and through their stories, they whispered to each other: Oh, it's just big enough to be an ordinary cock. But others whispered: No, it was actually that big when it was caught, but since then, it has shrunk. Is that really so, they marvelled back. Might have been better to catch it alive, some said. What was wrong with finishing it off, others asked. While they debated these things, they also shooed away the children who had come to take a peek. Though they had decided to bury it without delay, Kurup saar counselled them that it was not fair to bury it in the absence of Chaakku and Mammath. Chaakku had gone early in the morning to see someone off at the airport, and

Mammath had gone to town. When Kurup saar asked if they could wait for some more time, they all said fine, and then some of them went their own way. It was then that Maryamma came running, screaming and beating her breast. For a moment, everyone was perplexed. The terrible wail pushed through the crowd and collapsed on the dead fowl. She hugged it close and began to wail even louder. Kochukuttan quietly slipped behind the crowd.

When she began to hurl obscenities at the murderer's father and mother in the middle of her lament, Jaleel advised Kochukuttan to leave. Noticing that everybody was absorbed in Maryamma's crying and cussing, he sneaked back behind the panchayat well and walked on tiptoe till the raised ridge near the Pulikka family's property. He hauled himself up on it, and ran home through the yard.

The cock that Kochukuttan had killed belonged to Maryamma. It was a *nercha*-cock—raised as an offering to be sacrificed when her daughter Rosamma found a good match. Her brother Sunny told Kurup saar that they should investigate how the fellow who had been securely shut inside the hen-coop had ended up in Kochukuttan's hands. The search parties of last night had been clearly instructed not to open anybody's hen-coops. Sunny was afraid that the gross violation of that rule, this utterly cruel act, might drive his sister mad. Kurup saar was worried too. Whenever there was a wedding anywhere close by, Maryamma never failed to pray that her daughter should get married soon. And whenever someone died in the area, she would weep in fear, beseeching that she be spared until her little girl was wedded. It was terrible to think that such a fate may befall her.

Because they knew that taking back a *nercha*-fowl that had met with an inauspicious end would bring even worse portents, those who helped Maryamma get back home had to abandon the dead bird in front of the panchayat office. Nobody dared to think of the cock, which was constantly sanctified with prayers while alive and with tears after its death, as a meal! As for burying it, the fear was that it would blight the soil forever. As they glumly pondered this difficult situation, Sunny came up with a solution: 'Let the murderer bury it himself!'

Mea culpa, admitted Kochukuttan, mea maxima culpa. But he pleaded not guilty to just one charge: 'I did not catch it from the hen-coop, please believe me. I found it on a low-lying branch of the jackfruit tree near Naaniyamma's house.' Sunny alone would not believe him. The hen-coop was new; it was hard to believe that the cock could get out of it on its own. Then how?

'Sunny, let's find a solution to this right now?' suggested Mathai.

'This fellow's been dragged here from his house for precisely that purpose,' retorted Sunny, eyeing Kochukuttan angrily.

Knowing that he deserved the anger, Kochukuttan became even more compliant: 'Just tell me what to do. I'll do it right now.'

'This is a *nercha*-fowl. It can't be taken back home. Nor can it be buried anywhere nearby. You'll have to take it outside our area and get rid of it, or bury it in your own yard.'

Kochukuttan looked at Jaleel; Jaleel returned the glance. He lifted the dead bird and walked towards the narrow path to his house. Jaleel followed. Halfway there, they met the hunchbacked Anthonias. Seeing him hobble down the path, they stood with their backs pressed against the side of the path. He stopped and held out his hand.

'This …' Kochukuttan began to explain.

'I know …' said Anthonias.

He took the bird and threw it on his back as if it were a rag, clasped its legs firmly with his wrinkly fingers, and hobbled on.

After he had walked a couple of feet ahead, Kochukuttan wanted to turn and take a look, but he didn't feel brave enough.

The discussion about last night's search and the post-mortem of its failure was taking place at Chaakku's house.

Sunny could not bear it any longer; he stood up, seeking attention.

'That asshole killed my sister's *nercha*-fowl!'

Chaakku leaned forward to control Sunny's ire.

'We are discussing a very important matter here. Do not butt in like this.'

'So, my sister's loss is nothing to you?'

'Sunny, do you know it happened again in the school this morning? Is that nothing to you?'

Sunny held back his irritation.

Chaakku declared that discussing the death of a *nercha*-fowl was actually criminal under present circumstances, and Sunny pretended to cool down: 'Oh, I am not so bad!'

'No, that's not what my brother-in-law meant,' Krishnankutty comforted him.

'I'll be with you, even if I have to give my life,' Sunny said, his voice trembling with emotion.

'We need to think of next steps,' Kurup saar reminded them.

The locality had four temples, one church and a mosque. If the squawking interrupted the early morning nirmaalyam at the Devi temple, it also desecrated the night-time athaazhapuja at the Siva temple. And no one could say where it would strike next. There was a huge legal dispute between two factions for control over the church. The court had allowed one of the factions, which claimed to be the true owners, to pray there two days a week; all the remaining days were reserved for the other faction. The qurbana service of both factions was disrupted by the bird's vile cackling. Because each faction accused the other of being the hand behind this abomination, neither participated in the fowl-hunt.

It was the crowing and clucking that rent the air when flowers were being offered at the martyr's pavilion for Comrade Appukkuttan that rattled the communists. Perhaps the similarity between the offering of flowers and the puja in the temple provoked the reaction, surmised one of them. The local committee secretary responded to this ordinary comrade by declaring that this *aachaaram*, this established ritual that had been observed for so long, at every stage in the movement, could not be abolished. Besides, it had come to their attention that the same horrid cackle was heard when people tried to consult astrologers about their future, when husbands yelled at wives or beat them, when men indulged in post-orgasmic neglect of their wives or lovers, and when they bragged about their family's eminence. And thus it became evident that this pestilence was affecting not just the social lives of the local folk, but also their existence as individuals. That made things really serious.

It was also observed that during the fowl-hunt last night, they had not heard a single cock crow. This meant that even those roosters which crowed occasionally to escape boredom seemed to have forgotten how to do it. Someone pointed out that they should take into account these circumstances in which no one could really rebut a charge that the culprit was their own rooster. The others were also convinced of this. So what, now?

'Total annihilation!'

When Kurup saar said that in his soft but firm voice, the others could not but sink into a consensus.

Kochukuttan was in a moral dilemma over the situation that would arise when all the hens became either widows or orphans. Haltingly, he put the question to Kurup saar. When there was no reply, it was presented to Chaakku.

'True. But under such circumstances, should they not be willing to accept it? Isn't this the country we all live in, humans and animals? The *moola-mantra* of our nation, after all, is sacrifice.'

Because Kurup saar nodded his head to that, all the others followed.

Kochukuttan tried to broach the issue with a couple of young men, who were his friends, on the strength of a few bottles of toddy, but to no avail; they weren't going to taste his brew. Another chap pointed at a signboard in the toddy shop that said 'Do not discuss politics', and segued smoothly into a film song.

A census of roosters was undertaken. One-hundred-and-sixty-two of them in all. Of these, one-hundred-and-sixty were perfectly healthy. One had a limp, but it was healthy enough to limp after the hens. The other was always in deep slumber. He would wake up briefly and then go right back to sleep. Probably had no memory whatsoever of crowing or cackling even.

The day after the census, all the cocks were transformed into cooked meat. The curry was distributed in the spirit of celebration in the premises of the panchayat office. Even then, the fact that Naaniyamma's rooster was absent at the gathering lay undigested inside most people.

The very same day, the payment for Kochukuttan's visa reached Saudi.

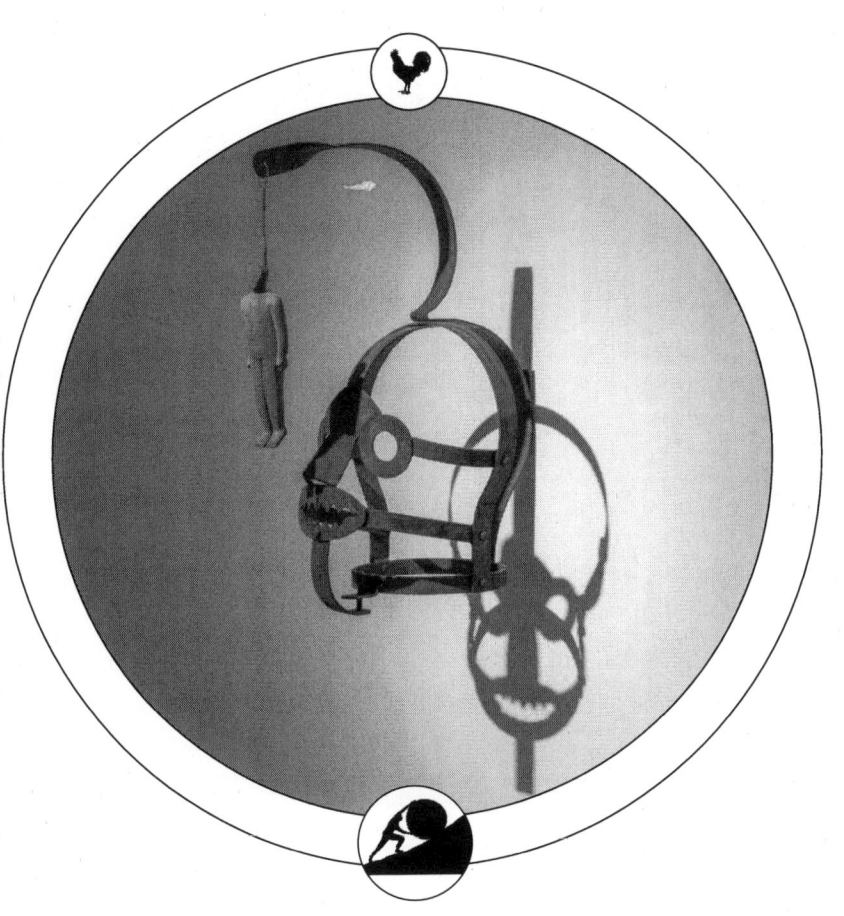

SEVEN

Ambiguity

Though no one could be blamed for the fact that the menace was unabated even after all the cocks had been butchered, the whisper that someone was hiding something crept all around.

In a meeting urgently called one morning, Chaakku raised a doubt that he considered crucial.

'What if it isn't a cock that's hooting?'

That was a suspicion that none of them had harboured even in their dreams.

'Couldn't this be a human being?'

Before they could consider the possibility, he continued, 'The only creature on earth that protests through sarcasm is the human being.'

'But, saar,' protested someone, 'how can a human being make such a racket?'

'Well, around the time I came to settle here after my marriage, I saw Vaasu the low-born uproot a thorny palm as tall as two full-grown men and run away with it! If someone who was less than four-and-a-half feet tall and thin as a rake could do that, this can happen too!'

Vaasu the velan was actually long gone. Both his daughters were good students and had done well in life. They were now employed far away, and their mother had followed them. They came back occasionally when their mother felt like seeing their old home again. She— Cheetheyi was her name—would visit some houses, but only through the backyard. The girls had told her sternly not to do so, but she would do just that. The last time she returned, the brahmin family in the Tekkedath Mana had given her food that was left over from lunch: some sambar and pulissery. The older girl had stopped the car when they were on their way back and flung it right back into the yard of the Mana. The younger girl had sworn never to come back there, and Cheetheyi had started to weep. The local asaan, the teacher who had taught the girls the alphabet on sand, was watching the confusion, and asked them, *enna* happened? Nothing, they said, and drove off. Since then, none of them had visited. No one knew if Cheetheyi was alive or dead.

'So ... you mean ...?'

'Yes … exactly …' Chaakku shifted in his chair and continued, 'We have to carry out another investigation.'

No relative of either Vaasu's or Cheetheyi's was around anywhere there. Then who, the others asked.

Chaakku found a solution for that. 'Let's make all the men here imitate a cock crowing.'

To those who doubted deep inside whether this wasn't absurd but were still silent, Chaakku offered this: 'Don't investigations make use of information about the size of the gap between teeth and the details of blood groups? What may sound like foolishness to us may actually help the investigation.'

Though many did not agree with this in the beginning, they began to yield, feeling that it was after all for a good cause—for the country. The believers who had been given permission to pray in the church two days a week announced that they wouldn't be available for the crowing demonstration; they walked out en masse. Despite many attempts to allay fears and assuage tempers, they did not relent. They gave way only when the unnerving cackle blasted the qurbana prayer held by the rival faction, who accused them of engineering it. So finally, they too swore to join the investigation.

The local sub-inspector of police was given the responsibility for holding the crowing demonstration. He was to examine the demonstrations for resemblance with the recorded version of the pesky cock's crowing.

When someone asked whether people couldn't fake a tone, Chaakku answered with a laugh, 'You don't know how criminals are caught!'

Into such ignorance, he poured details of how criminals were nabbed in America. Kochukuttan realised that Chaakku was drawing heavily on Hollywood movies, but stayed quiet. Hearing him refer to the Guantanamo prison and Mexican immigrants, many were impressed.

It was Oommen saar who had taught him how important it was to be wary of people shoving primitive ideas in your face while science was making so much progress. That was exactly what was happening here. Because he could not put up a one-man fight, Kochukuttan resolved to meet Oommen saar in secret the next day and tell him all. And so he went to his house early the next morning. Before he could even mention his misgivings, Oommen saar said, 'I know what's going on.'

'Isn't it a pity, saar?' Kochukuttan asked.

'If you ask me, yes. Many others also agree.'

Oommen saar's reference to 'many others' was a straw that Kochukuttan was ready to seize upon. 'Who all, saar?'

'Many—that's it—just know that many others feel the same. Just that they aren't saying it out loud.'

'Isn't that a terrible pity, saar?'

'Yes, indeed. But they're all people of high standing. They aren't going to do anything that will disturb their peace of mind.'

'You can say it, saar …?'

Oommen saar smiled briefly.

'My dear Kochu, I did quite a bit of that in my youth. I am tired now. Also, my younger daughter just had a baby. Molly and I are leaving for the US tomorrow.'

Ah, but saar, still … Kochukuttan was trying to voice his disappointment when saar grabbed him by the hand and took him inside the house, saying that it was a very good thing he had come by that morning because two of the bathroom taps had stopped working.

Though Chaakku claimed that the cock's crowing had been recorded perfectly, he did not reveal when, where and how that had happened. No one asked him, either. Public announcements were made that all adult males of voting age in the panchayat were to assemble at the government primary school from eight o'clock in the morning on the following Sunday. Kochukuttan was given the responsibility of bringing all the infirm males to the school as a penance for slaughtering the *nercha*-cock. He did not complain.

The police arrived that morning and had a sumptuous breakfast at Chaakku's house. The lunch menu had been supplied well in advance to Babu, the curry-chef at the toddy shop: fresh fish from the river, shrimp from the lake, pork, toddy from the famous toddy shop at Thollaayiram, tapioca steamed plain, tapioca cooked in spices and crushed coconut paste, then doused with fresh coconut oil and garnished with curry leaves. Chaakku instructed the servers that if toddy wasn't acceptable, rum or whisky could be served instead of warm water. And it was easy to pass off the booze as water, because warm water boiled with Karingali powder has a rich brown tint. That made it more convenient (than toddy given away by its whitish pallor). Just a working lunch, not a booze-party, it would look like. Krishnankutty was given overall charge of the meal.

Chaakku did the cock-crowing-imitation first. Then came Kurup. Till noon, there was not even a hint of a resemblance. All that one could hear were ugly sounds from weak human throats reverberating in the classrooms.

When they sat down for lunch, the sub-inspector asked Chaakku, 'Is this going to end up as a foolish joke?'

'No,' Chaakku assured him.

Downing the well-cooked pork, he posed a fresh query to Chaakku, hoping to draw on the latter's wealth of experience. 'Has such an incident ever happened in the history of India?'

Chaakku could not tell whether he was referring to the continuous assaults of the cock or to the present experimental investigation.

'The experimental investigation,' the sub-inspector clarified.

'Isn't this how history is made?' Chaakku beamed as he replied.

The policemen rested a while after lunch. The mimicry continued. By evening, only two men were left: Kochukuttan and Anthonias.

'Kochukuttan is taking Kollangara Madhavan chettan back home. He'll be back soon,' someone hollered.

'And Anthonias?' asked Kurup saar.

No one replied.

'Not likely to come,' Mathai quipped.

'Let Kochukuttan go and get him,' Chaakku said.

Anthonias had arrived here as a fugitive at the age of twenty, after having stabbed someone at the annual feast of the Church of the Three Kings. It was Kochukuttan's father who had given him refuge, protecting him from the police for a whole week. When it came to be known that the victim was not going to pursue the case, Anthonias went back to his native place. One Sunday, he cut down the bell of the church and hung a cow's ripped-out innards in its place. The blood dripping from it soaked the rope and it began to stink. This time, the local folk actually drowned him in the Minachil river. He dived into the inner currents, gathered up his last breath, and made for the shore. Again, Kochukuttan's father came to his rescue. There was a rumour that Anthonias, who shunned the church, was a Satan-worshipper. People said that if his eyes fell on a pregnant woman, the foetus would dissipate and die on the third day. Sumathi, who was pregnant with Kochukuttan at the time, had served him rice-gruel in their house, declaring coolly that if that was so, let it happen.

'He'll come only if you call,' Kurup saar insisted.

Though he was a friend of his father's, Anthonias had not spoken with Kochukuttan even once. And because he had heard so many terrifying tales about Anthonias since childhood, Kochukuttan too had never tried talking to him.

After he left to get Anthonias, the people gathered there experienced a twinge of cold fear. They beat a retreat, so they wouldn't have to listen to the terrible cackle that was likely to rise from his throat.

People were making sure that his eyes didn't fall on them. Only the police and Chaakku were left behind. The same troubled breath rose and fell at the same pace in all the bodies gathered there. As each moment passed, they felt fatigued. Even after Kochukuttan had left with Anthonias in a car, no one dared to step into the school yard.

But then, finally, the resemblance revealed itself. The people there now knew of the similarity between Kochukuttan's crowing and that of the rooster. The place, and all the people there, collectively woke up to an immense night they could never fathom.

EIGHT

The Room

Sunny went up to Maryamma, who hadn't left her bed since the sad demise of her *nercha*-fowl, and reported: 'Chedathy, get up! It was that scoundrel—Sumathi's son—who was crowing like a cock everywhere!'

Maryamma leapt up. 'And where is that son of a whore now?'

'The police took him.'

She swung around to snap at Rosamma who, on hearing Sunny's words, had exclaimed that that was really unfair.

It was a room in which many different kinds of light fell. In the middle of it was a fully bloomed flower with a man seated on it. His cock was stiff, and a serpent was sucking it. He was caressing its head gently. It enjoyed the caress and lay still and obedient. There was a gun in his right hand with which he was taking aim. A naked young man stood facing the mouth of the gun. I am innocent, I have done no wrong, he was saying, but his voice was drowned deep inside him, tied to a boulder. The sounds of the crowd waiting outside to see him die were deployed inside the room along with the lights. The young man sensed that all those who stood on his side were whispering through their breath: we are innocent, we are innocent. The gun's aim shifted towards an old man, and he collapsed, screaming. Which country does he belong to, the soldiers yelled, asking the crowd outside. The speculators in the crowd broke into groups and shouted back—Palestine, Syria, Myanmar …

Before the name of the country of the accused was announced, Kochukuttan screamed aloud.

'This is common when you have a high fever,' the doctor said. Only Sumathi, Jaleel and Jaleel's mother were near him. Kochukuttan's eyes were rolling wildly, and he was ranting and raving.

Outside, the doctor told Chaakku and the policemen, 'He'll have to be admitted here for two or three days.'

The sub-inspector reminded them that it was the duty of Chaakku and other eminent citizens to protect Kochukuttan from being lynched by a mob when he returned from the hospital.

'If anyone tries to clobber him again, he'll probably die. Make sure nothing happens to him.'

Chaakku shook his head in agreement.

Kochukuttan was discharged on the second day. The road was full of people on both sides. There was much hooting, jeering and cussing as the car that carried him somehow made its way to the lane that led to his house. Jaleel and Sumathi followed them with the utensils and sheets they had taken to the hospital.

As Kochukuttan took a step holding on to his mother's shoulder, a stone hit Jaleel from behind. Krishnankutty, Kurup and others were shouting at the crowd to not throw stones, but they kept coming. Before Kochukuttan could get into the frontyard of his house, Maryamma dashed up, spat on his face, and rained obscenities on his grandfathers going back many generations. Mathai and two others grabbed and pulled her out of the way; the sharp kitchen-knife she had hidden under her upper cloth slashed Mathai's thumb.

A large crowd, both invited and uninvited, milled around Chaakku's house, and so the meeting had to be shifted to the Nair Karayogam hall. People of all castes and creeds sat together, enjoying the breeze from the new ceiling fans that Chaakku had recently donated. They had gathered there to discuss the next steps.

A general observation was made that in the two days after Kochukuttan was nabbed, there had been no untoward incidents of cock-crowing at all. But the astrologer Varma said that, just the other day, he had definitely heard it while setting his kavadi-counters for a prediction. The priest of the temple of Padinjhattil also reported that the crowing was still a nuisance at the nightly worship of attaazhapuja. Chaakku dismissed both accounts as mere figments of the imagination. Though there was general agreement that they should be thinking of future steps, no one knew what those were.

NINE

The Illness

Kesavan Vaidyar, the healer, looked at Kochukuttan through his blurry cataract-ridden eyes for some time. Then, closing his eyes thoughtfully, he said, 'This illness will last lifelong. Medicines will help. But it will never be fully healed.'

Sidhhmam Rooksha bahihsnigdhamantharkhrshtam rajaha kirel/shlakshnasparsham tanushwetataamram daugdhi- kapushpaval praayena chordhvakaaye syaal gandhai.

The healer recited this shloka and opened his eyes. *Sidhmam*. A form of leprosy. It will be extreme on the outside and soft and moist inside. Any abrasions from itching or otherwise will cause it to break open. It will be smooth and thin to the touch. It will be of a whitish, coppery brown colour, like the chura-flower. It will manifest as a reddish rash, which will itch moderately.

'Don't be scared by the word leprosy. In Ayurveda, all skin diseases are *kushtam*—leprosy,' said the vaidyar. 'This may afflict you because of sins committed in past births or this one. Also from consuming foods that don't agree with each other. It could also be because of the harm done to good folk, or stealing things that belong to others.'

Kochukuttan was drained in body and mind like never before. He tried to ask the vaidyar something, tongue slurring, but a wave of unexpected tears rose up and drowned the effort.

'Fear, anxiety—these make it worse. You must do everything possible to restore mental peace—prayer or meditation, or whatever.'

Kochukuttan could only sob; he did not respond.

His terror circled the constricting space of his room, panting desperately like a cornered blind dog. Am I in this mess because of past sins, like the vaidyar said, he asked himself. Earlier, if anyone said that masturbation was a sin, he would argue with them not just for any number of hours, but over any number of days. Why do you say so? What exactly is wrong with it? It doesn't hurt anyone. It does not assault anyone. The only bad thing about it is that you may fantasise taking the girl you fancy on the school bench or in the shed or the attic—places unfit for human copulation. He had fantasised about fucking Rema, the girl who came to gather arrowroot, on a bed of dry leaves in the rubber-tree patch behind the temple. Kochukuttan could come only when the small talk of people coming to the temple through the patch, the sound of the bells at the time of the evening worship and the sharp scent of the over-burned wicks in the stone-lamps there commingled with the rubber sap and surrounded him. Likewise, desire took people to many yards, attics, and other such places. The mahout Sreedharan's second wife was regularly called to the attic of the coconut-barn of the brahmin homestead, the Tekkedathu Mana. When she climbed the stairs, the curtain that was her mundu would rise and fall over her calves evenly, as though weaving something. It seemed steeped in the pleasure of that rhythmic act. And then they would roll inside, and the coconuts would shake and shiver, and there would be quite a party up there. That's when Kochukuttan would climax.

Rema was in the yard picking the arrowroot. His gaze, which had got past the thin window-bars without his permission, seemed to be gasping mildly. He closed his eyes and lay still for some time. Was this disease the cost he was paying for every woman he had subjected to his sexual fantasies? Kochukuttan looked at his penis. Its tip was a mouldy white colour and looked diseased.

A cock to be sacrificed to Goddess Karthyayani of the Cherthala temple, toddy and fowls for the Malayaraya

sacred grove at Mundakkayam, a small silver miniature of
a cock for the temple of Karikulangara—Sumathi's friend
Remani was trying to persuade her to make all these vows.

Sumathi told her, 'You know quite well that I have
never gone to a temple, and I don't believe in any of it—
and still you tell me all this?'

Remani jumped up and clamped Sumathi's mouth
with her hand. 'Oh, someone may hear you!'

'So what?' Sumathi asked.

'Don't say that,' Remani begged. 'This is for our boy.'

Sumathi did not respond. The ezhavas, parayas,
pulayas, velans, and all the other labouring castes in the
village had built their homes at the edge of the paddy fields
towards the western side. Hard to call it 'home'—'a small
shelter inside a makeshift shed' was a better description.
Because all the temples in this place were for the Nairs
and the Nambuthiris—the Malayali brahmins—to pray
and while away their time chatting, the other castes didn't
go that way. The Temple Entry Proclamation had made
it possible for people of all castes to enter temples. But
Sumathi's father did not believe in a life lived in debt
to the gods. 'Work hard, and you can eat. Now, if you
sit around praying, that's not going to happen,' he had
told her ever since she was a child. Sumathi had told
Kochukuttan the same thing. And so, the gods did not
reign inside him ever.

I can't be bothered to go to the temples I have never gone to, even for my boy, she resolved.

When she went to his room with rice-gruel after some time, Kochukuttan was shivering uncontrollably.

She called Jaleel. Kochukuttan was howling about the prison-rooms that appeared in his eyes whenever he shut them.

Jaleel tried to calm him down, but every little sound outside felt like the footsteps of the police to Kochukuttan.

They gave him a tablet the healer had prescribed. That let him sleep for a while. When Jaleel stepped out of the room, he saw, for the first time in his life, Kochukuttan's mother weep. She, who was totally unshaken by her husband's death and the challenge of raising her son all alone. Jaleel did not know how to console her. After some time, she gathered her strength again and told him, 'Please find out about his passport.'

Yes, Jaleel nodded.

TEN

The Mother

*J*aleel met Kurup saar and begged him to go and see Kochukuttan at least once. Kurup saar said that it wasn't right to be speaking with an accused. When Jaleel persisted, he took the matter to Chaakku and others. They did not agree at first, but then Kurup saar held up a much-used example—was it not a jungle-dweller, an uncivilised man, who later became the great rishi Valmiki, he asked them. They agreed to this, but some were still suspicious about why he wanted to meet Kurup saar.

'You must ask him something,' said Chaakku, 'something that he did not reveal even when the police questioned him.'

'What?' Kurup saar asked.

'Isn't Naaniyamma's rooster still missing?'

'So?'

84

'That rooster is very dangerous,' Chaakku said, lowering his voice. 'If this chap is locked up in jail, it will be impossible to catch the other fellow. If Kochukuttan is outside, they will communicate with each other. So we must persuade him to give up the rooster. The way to do it is to promise that the case against him will be withdrawn. Before that, we need to give him a test dose to see if he will indeed transform into Valmiki.'

'How?

'That Ramachandran will give you,' said Chaakku.

Kurup saar told Jaleel to bring Kochukuttan to his house early the next morning. Kochukuttan was terrified of stepping out of the house, but Jaleel reassured him.

They sat on the steps leading to the river just behind Kurup saar's house. This was the conversation that followed: Why did you do it? My dearest saar, I swear upon my mother, I was not the one who crowed. When the police and Chaakku announce that you did it, with evidence, wouldn't people believe it? What can I do to stop them from thinking that now? First of all, get rid of this beard and long hair; look decent. Today or tomorrow someone will come for a detailed investigation. Isn't it necessary to look respectable? That's why I am telling you this. Aren't a beard and long hair respectable, saar? This is the trouble with you—before anything else, stop asking such questions. But it's you who taught us that we should always question everything. That was in the old days. If we get into trouble now, there'll be nobody to help us. And so, what is to be done? Just keep quiet, basically. You know that this isn't a simple police case? Saar, you must not frighten me like this; as it is, I can't sleep. I am not frightening you, just pointing out the reality. So what am I to do, saar? First, tell me, where is Naaniyamma's rooster? My dearest saar, I haven't even seen it! Really? Then why did you go and challenge Chaakku with a sense of social justice we've never seen in you before? Saare, she is a helpless woman, isn't she? That's why I went over to find out. If you tell us where that cock is, you'll escape. But saar, for that I should know where it is! Calm yourself, and think carefully. Eda, does Naaniyamma know that you are suffering for her sake—no, right? Then, whose loss is it? Yours and your family's, correct? So think about all that I've said. And before you go, take this photo with you and put it in front of your house for now. Everything else, we will resolve when we come to it. Yes, saar.

Seeing a photo on the wall of the verandah on her way back from a bath, Sumathi asked Kochukuttan, 'Eda, who's this?'

'That's … the … Matha … the Mother …'

86

'Eh? I am your matha, as far as I know.'

'No ... yes, this ...'

'One matha will do for this house. Get rid of this one.'

'No, but ...'

'Just listen to me. Where's the photo of Sree Narayana Guru which used to be here?'

'It's in the room.'

'Bring it back and hang it here.'

'Let this stay here too ...?'

'No.'

Kochukuttan consecrated the Guru on the wall again.

'Also, put back behind it, the grocer's credit-book, the matchbox, the candle, and the receipt of the chitty-savings man.'

He obeyed her fully. Throwing a pained look at Kochukuttan, who was now without his hair and beard, Sumathi went inside.

ELEVEN

The Hens

People pooled money to replace the dead birds. New roosters reached the homes of those who had lost them. Many found out that these birds often crowed at the wrong hours. Kurup saar felt that this was only to be expected because the birds had to adjust to their new surroundings. His statement was enough to allay doubts. But the newcomers were perturbed by the resistance of the hens, who would not accept them as their new husbands. Many of them sank into depression. Many stopped crowing altogether. Some just went away. Some managed to consume food that no fowl had ever eaten, and killed themselves. In just a week, all the new cocks were gone.

Ramachandran demanded that Kochukuttan's role in misleading the hens who, till now, had lived a decent life of pecking and laying eggs and raising chickens be investigated.

Kurup saar also thought that this was a very valid demand.

'There's an attempt to arm hens who have been widowed. The new cocks were brought here taking into account the loneliness and the widowed state of the hens (who ought to have been proud of the martyred cocks), but they have not been cooperative. There is a conspiracy behind it, and so the evil fate that befell those roosters portends even greater evil,' he reminded.

Though Kurup saar was uncertain about the exact nature of the conspiracy, Chaakku was quite sure. He was willing to share it with that small audience on the condition that it should not be transmitted to another ear. Everyone agreed.

'In two days, it will be the fifteenth of August.'

'So?'

'Kochukuttan is now outside. Naaniyamma's cock is also out there, on the loose.' Chaakku smiled as he spoke.

This awfully vague talk that seemed to disagree and agree with everything at the same time sent everyone into confusion. At this time, someone came over to Kurup saar and whispered something in his ear. Because it was rude to be sharing secrets when one was with others, Kurup saar said it aloud: 'Kochukuttan has not pasted Matha's photo on the wall of his house.'

Chaakku drew upon his own experience to prove that that if someone deliberately fritters away an occasion to prove their love for the nation, there must be deep anti-national sentiment piled up inside them. 'There's a power behind Kochukuttan, much bigger than you think.' That stopped everybody's breath for a split-second.

It returned only when Damodara Menon began to speak in his mildly stuttering voice. When he said that he had heard the crowing that morning while he was wiping clean Indiraji's photograph and garlanding it, Chaakku tried to dismiss it as usual, saying that it was just a feeling. But Menon did not give up. 'How can that be?' he asked. 'That's the psychology,' Chaakku argued. 'When we hear something for a very long time, even when it ends, the echoes remain. All those who are still hearing the cock crow are experiencing that echo in their unconscious.' Menon approved of Chaakku's psychological explanation. But then, another, more serious question was raised.

'Isn't it easy for someone who can prepare even hens for an armed rebellion to escape from here?'

Chaakku laughed and said, 'His passport application has been rejected in the police verification procedure. So how is he going to escape?'

'Maybe into the jungle?'

'You know perfectly well what happens to people who disappear into the forests.'

No one had a quick reply to that. Many faces rose up in the memories that sprang within each brain present there. Some people did feel uncomfortable. But they kept quiet. A sense of jubilation reared itself up lustily inside most of them, like a full-blooded man drawing himself up to his full height.

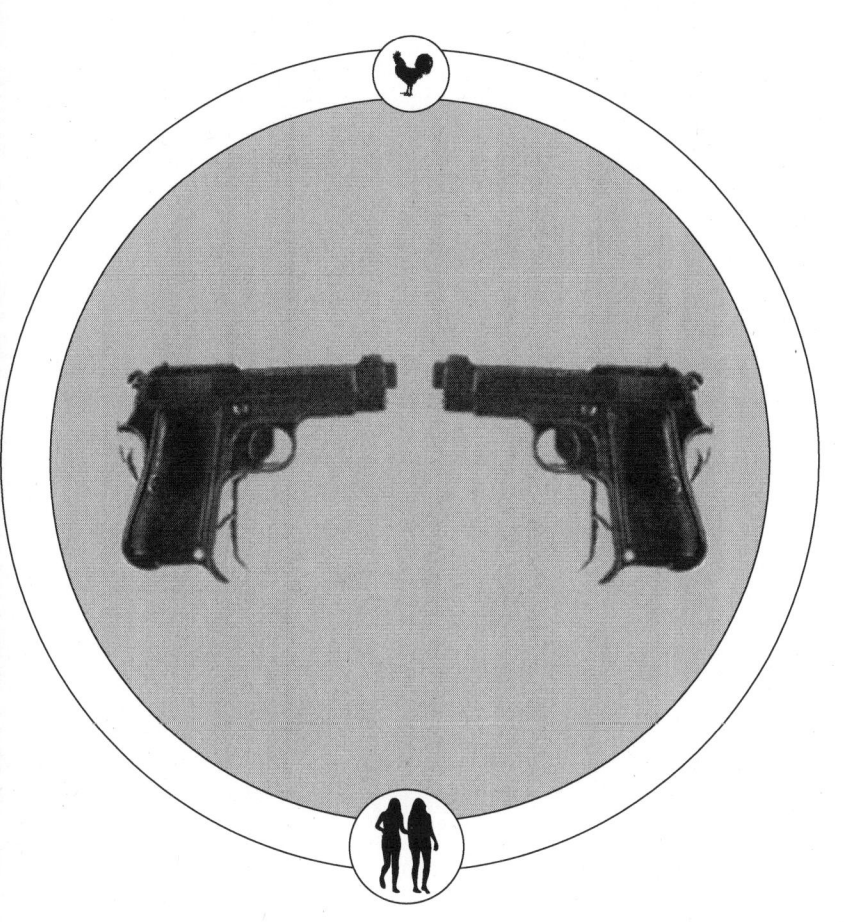

TWELVE

The Trial

*B*ecause all hearts are not equally capable of holding secrets, the valve of somebody's heart gave way, and the secret escaped. And it reached Jaleel's ears. He reached Kochukuttan's bedside even before he had heard it fully. Kochukuttan was trying to clean out his bowels with a dose of Avipathi powder. Seeing how weak he was, Jaleel thought better of telling him that he was going to be in danger on the fifteenth of August. He got up to leave, thinking that the news might take away whatever life was left in his body.

He knew that there were good marksmen in the eastern parts. His Maama had told him about Paappu Mappila, an employee in his shop, who went hunting blindfolded. And that's how Jaleel decided to approach him.

'Won't some poison do to finish off a cock?' Mappila asked.

'This is no ordinary cock,' Jaleel clarified. 'You can only hear it, not see it. If it starts to crow when the flag is hoisted, then that's the end of my friend's life.'

Mappila spread some lime on a tobacco leaf and pushed it into his molar. He just couldn't fathom how someone's life would end if a cock crowed. People had got him to shoot wild pigs and bison. This was the first time someone wanted him to shoot a cock. At first, he thought that it was a joke. But after hearing Jaleel out, he was convinced that this was an unusual bird.

'How's the terrain?' he asked.

'It's sort of hilly, with ups and downs. There's some rubber, and lots of small lanes and terraces.'

'So mostly like this place, isn't it?'

Jaleel looked around and said, 'Yes, somewhat.'

Mappila spat out the juice of the tobacco and asked him everything he knew about the places in which the rooster was heard, the distance between one such place and another, the houses around the school where the flag-hoisting was to happen, the kinds of trees around there, and so on. Jaleel, who regularly delivered newspapers there, was able to sketch out the geography of the area pretty quickly. Mappila walked through the whole area mentally and told him: 'We need six men with guns.'

Jaleel nodded.

'We will reach early at dawn on the fifteenth. The men will have to identify their spots before daylight. We can't shoot at sight. A creature that hides mysteriously should be tackled with stealth.'

Jaleel didn't understand much of what the Mappila said, but he agreed to be at the junction before daybreak. As he was stepping out, he asked, 'How much will all this cost?'

'You are Saidutty's relative—so just the money for the jeep ride.'

When Jaleel turned into the lane that went to Kochukuttan's house, he saw two strangers ahead of him. When he increased his pace, one of them turned around and stopped. Jaleel slowed down. They stood there waiting for him.

'Are you Jaleel?' one of them asked.

He nodded yes.

'We are going to see Kochukuttan. If you are also going there, then better come after some time.'

Jaleel told them hesitantly that he did not recognise them. They did not respond; just smiled and walked off. When they reached his house, Kochukuttan was sitting on his bed, leaning against its headboard. They went straight into his room, without knocking. That scared him. When they did not see any chairs there, one of them, the fat one, went and got two chairs from the verandah.

'You are very tired, aren't you?' the bald one asked.

Kochukuttan only nodded.

Seeing the skin peeling off Kochukuttan's hands, the fat one asked, 'Is this psoriasis?'

'Yes,' Kochukuttan replied.

'Some people get this when they get tense. That must be how you got it?'

'Yes,' he said.

'What reason do you have to be so full of mental tension?'

Kochukuttan did not say anything.

'Edo, you are the only son in the family. You drink a few bottles of toddy occasionally. And once you get the visa, you are going to find a job outside. Just tell us: Why should such a fellow suffer from any tension?'

'Because ...' Kochukuttan paused for a moment and then continued. 'I've been accused of something I didn't even know of. The truth is that I didn't do it. I have been very afraid, and that made me ill.'

The bald man pulled his chair closer and said, 'In that case, you just need to firmly say that you did not do it.'

'Saare, they don't believe me when I say that.'

'That's really awful, isn't it, saare?' The bald man looked at the fat one.

The fat one agreed. 'It's not right to trap someone. Are they trying to trap you? What do you feel?'

'That's what I think.'

'What did you study?'

'Plumbing.'

'Plumbing is a great line! In more demand than medical practice!' He laughed.

'Are your parents alive?'

'My father is no more; I have my mother.'

'What did your father do for a living?'

'He had a shop. My mother is a tailor in a shop in town.'

'Do you go to the temple?'

'No.'

'Are you devout?'

'No, not very.'

'Edo, see, if we are pious, we won't do wrong things,' said the bald man.

'But I haven't done any wrong things, saare.'

They laughed.

'Okay, whatever. Now, which is your favourite country?'

'I have no favourites. I like them all.'

'The ideal of the universal citizen, right?'

Kochukuttan did not respond.

'That's a good ideal. Few at your age have the ability to even think of it. But is it proper that someone with such ideals once went around singing songs derogatory to one of those nations?'

'No, it's not.'

'Do you know the song *Saare Jahan Se Achcha*?'

'Yes.'

'Do you know how it's parodied? I mean the one that replaces "achcha" with "father"—achchan? *Saare, this is my Achchan. His name is Kuttan Pillai ...* Is it right to sing such a song?'

'No.'

'Didn't you sing this when you were a student of class three?'

For a moment, Kochukuttan was at a loss.

'Tell us the truth. Did you not sing it?'

'I don't remember, saare.'

The bald man pulled out a piece of paper from his pocket, saying, 'Oh, there are people around here who remember.'

'Do you remember this bank account?'

'It's mine,' Kochukuttan agreed with a nod of his head.

'Who's this Yasin Muhammed who received one lakh and fifty thousand from you?'

'He's the person who is arranging my visa.'

'Who is he, I asked.'

'He's an acquaintance of my friend, Ashraf. Ashraf and I studied together.'

'Whose are these numbers that we found in your phone?' The two men showed him the call list.

'Those are Ashraf's.'

'Doesn't he have a mobile or a landline?'

'He has a mobile phone, but he always calls from this number.'

'Did you think you wouldn't be traced if you called through the Internet?'

Kochukuttan looked at them helplessly.

'Why did you get rid of your hair and beard and change your appearance?'

'I wasn't changing my appearance.'

They hmm-ed and stood up. Kochukuttan struggled to get up, but they said, 'No, just lie there.'

Before they stepped out, they turned around and asked him once more: 'What did you say your friends' names were? Jaleel and Ashraf, right?'

Not able to comprehend the import of that question, Kochukuttan stared at them blankly.

When it was past evening, Sumathi heard a huge scream run furiously along the road. She hurried there. Some people were running after it. Before long, she got to know that Maryamma's daughter Rosamma had eloped.

Many hurried back home to check if their sons and men were present. Some called home to make sure; yet others sent someone to see. Once it was confirmed that the number of men tallied, they went out again, curious to know who Rosamma had eloped with.

As this curiosity encircled Maryamma's house, Rosamma's brother Sunny found a note under her pillow. It said: 'Sindhu and I have decided to live together.'

THIRTEEN

War

Jaleel waited for Paappu Mappila on the verandah of a shop at the roadside junction. It was very dark. After half an hour, a one-eyed jeep came growling up.

'Let's go,' Jaleel said.

'Get in the back,' Mappila said.

One of the occupants of the backseat lifted a buttock and Jaleel squeezed himself into the gap. They first went to the Devi temple. Jaleel told them that there was a clump of rubber trees behind it. Mappila grunted. Jaleel had no clue how they were going to get a grip on the place; everything looked the same in the dark. But Mappila grunted like he could see everything in the dark. Once he had marked each place with his grunts, he said that they must go back to the rubber-tree patch. One of the men switched on his headlamp, and its beam cut through the thickly wooded place, sharper than an arrow. He followed it. The other men took their positions.

Before Paappu Mappila went off after them, Jaleel said to him, 'Please save us.'

'He'll be down the moment he opens his beak, don't worry,' he reassured Jaleel. 'You take courage, son.'

Chaakku had been worried that Maryamma's daughter's elopement would affect the flag-hoisting. But it was clear that his fears were unfounded. The school ground was full of people.

Chaakku was handing over the new flag that he had donated to the school. The headmaster received it with great regard, but then he began to tremble. He had noticed a face at the head of the crowd. He struggled not to drop the flag. His sudden transformation puzzled Chaakku for a moment, but he followed the headmaster's eyes and saw Kochukuttan standing there. Chaakku didn't tremble. He merely hid his distaste and requested the headmaster to hoist the flag.

As people proudly watched the tricolour rise slowly into the freedom of the skies, Kochukuttan's heart pounded for fear of that loud crowing that may burst out any moment. But then, all of a sudden, the sound of gunshots rent the air, shaking up the crowd. All the faces that were turned towards the flag now swung to where the sound of the gunshots had come from. After a few moments of stunned silence, Chaakku was the first to run. The rest of the crowd took to their heels after him. When everybody ran, the headmaster's hand and mind failed him.

Kochukuttan lowered himself beneath the flagpole, looking worn out and haggard. That's when he saw a rooster saunter by.

'Are you Naaniyamma's guy?' he asked him.

The rooster threw him a bewitching smile with a shake of his bright rainbow-coloured tail.

Paappu Mappila and his friends, defeated by a mere rooster, also made themselves scarce without even taking the money for their jeep ride.

Translator's Note

The Cock is the Culprit is a gossipy tale set in the tiny universe of a Kerala village. Unni's narratorial voice, as in his earlier work, fluctuates between female and male versions of gossipy and provincial talk—gossip being a weapon of choice for the weak, male or female. The state, as in his earlier stories, is distant, forbidding; the police is easily given to torturing the weak and pandering to the powerful. Love of the nation, when it appears in a tiny village circle far away from the centre of the nation, appears decidedly forced and comic, and is ultimately a false emotion that makes greed and crime look respectable. Aligned against it is the force of local ties and friendships that cut across religious lines. Unni's tale is about how powerful men— those who wield and weaponise patriarchal nationalist and community identities—grow unnerved when the persistent crowing of an unknown rooster disrupts their everyday moments of self-affirmation.

But the translator actively seeks out other subtexts that she must do justice to as well. That I have chosen to translate the title of the novel, *Prathi Poovankozhi*, into *The Cock is the Culprit*, and not *The Rooster is the Culprit*, is no coincidence. In Malayalam, *poovankozhi* stands for cocky masculinity and power, but in English, it does not do so. 'Cock', however, instantly calls up the phallus and its power. This is to do justice to the powerful subtext that makes this book utterly remarkable. In the translation, I use both words, according to context. For the Malayalam word *prathi*, I have deliberately chosen the word 'culprit' over 'defendant' or 'accused' because of its unique history—it once presumed that the court would pronounce the person subjected to trial guilty when they denied the crime.

There is an undeniably gendered—queer—subtext to this: the rooster is indeed the cock, one that is unseen, only heard, and which sends the hyper-masculine into irrational panic, and queer because the 'cock' in question does not belong to the masculine at all; it has no shape discernible to the eye, only a mocking sound that cannot be captured in human language, the pure power of disruption. Indeed, the villagers, the police, the local moneyed villain, all zero in on a complete 'outsider' as its owner: a nonagenarian hearing-impaired single woman living on her own, who, however, was named after an elusive revolutionary famous for giving the authorities the slip. And in the mêlée and confusion around the cock's alleged sarcastic cackling, a young woman gives the heteronormative order the slip, eloping with her female lover. The circle of masculine power includes the hyper-nationalist Hindus, the leaderships of minority communities and the communists. All of them are interrupted by bursts of derisive cackling, allegedly by the unseen cock—and are unable to climax—in their ceremonies of self-affirmation. And when the cock finally reveals itself to Kochukuttan, it is indeed a dandy of a rooster, flashing rainbow colours. *The Cock is the Culprit* is not only about Hindutva nationalism as some have suggested; it's also about the patriarchal micro-fascism that infects all social life in Kerala.

It is a cautionary tale too. The young lower-caste working-class man who tried to take on the upper-caste predatory villain learns the hard way that a direct fight is fruitless. Flight seems to be the only way out, as the two young women who survive show.

I thank Unni for letting me translate his work and Minakshi Thakur for her careful reading of the text and many thoughtful queries that have made this work so much more pleasurable. Thanks are due, also, to the many readers of *One Hell of a Lover* whose encouragement has been valuable indeed.